Parents and Caregivers,

Stone Arch Readers are designed to provide enjoyable reading experiences, as well as opportunities to develop vocabulary, literacy skills, and comprehension. Here are a few ways to support your beginning reader:

- Talk with your child about the ideas addressed in the story.

- Discuss each illustration, mentioning the characters, where they are, and what they are doing.

- Read with expression, pointing to each word. You may want to read the whole story through and then revisit parts of the story to ensure that the meanings of words or phrases are understood.

- Talk about why the character did what he or she did and what your child would do in that situation.

- Help your child connect with characters and events in the story.

Remember, reading with your child should be fun, not forced. Each moment spent reading with your child is a priceless investment in his or her literacy life.

Gail Saunders-Smith, Ph.D.

STONE ARCH **READERS**

are published by Stone Arch Books
A Capstone Imprint
1710 Roe Crest Drive
North Mankato, Minnesota 56003
www.capstonepub.com

Library of Congress Cataloging-in-Publication Data
Suen, Anastasia.
Dino hunt : a Robot and Rico story / by Anastasia Suen ; illustrated by Mike Laughead.
p. cm. — (Stone Arch readers)
ISBN 978-1-4342-1870-4 (library binding)
ISBN 978-1-4342-2300-5 (pbk.)
[1. Dinosaurs—Fiction. 2. Games—Fiction. 3. Museums—Fiction. 4. Robots—Fiction.]
I. Laughead, Mike, ill. II. Title.
PZ7.S94343Di 2010
[E]—dc22
2009034209

Summary: Robot and Rico go to the museum and take part in a scavenger hunt.

Art Director: Bob Lentz
Graphic Designer: Hilary Wacholz

Reading Consultants:
Gail Saunders-Smith, Ph.D.
Melinda Melton Crow, M.Ed.
Laurie K. Holland, Media Specialist

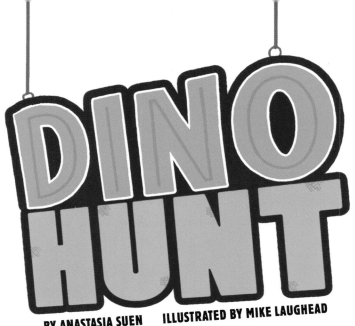

DINO HUNT

BY ANASTASIA SUEN   ILLUSTRATED BY MIKE LAUGHEAD

A ROBOT AND RICO STORY

STONE ARCH BOOKS
a capstone imprint

This is ROBOT.
Robot has lots of tools.

He uses the tools to help his
best friend, RICO.

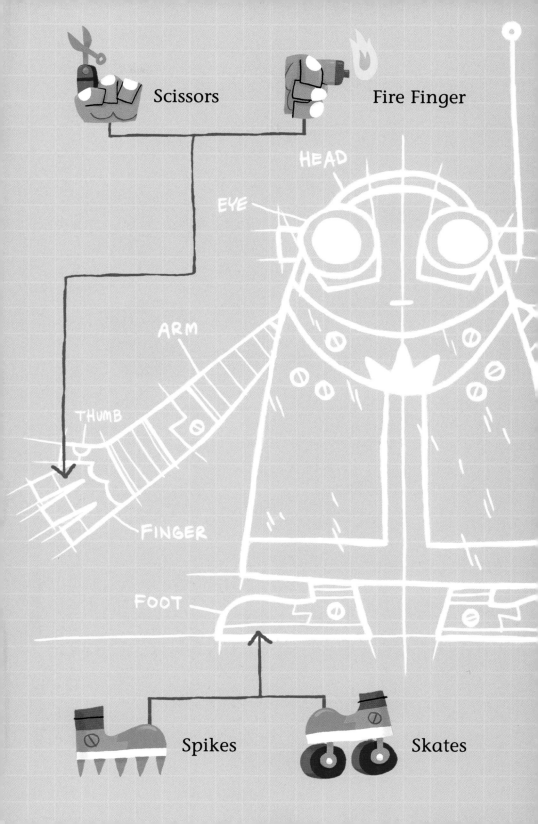

Robot and Rico go to the museum.

"What is that?" asks Rico.

"It's a game," says Robot. "We have to look for things that match these words."

"I can do it," says Rico.

"So can I," says Robot. "Let's work as a team."

"Where will we start?" asks Rico.

Robot looks at the list.

"The first word on the list is
old," says Robot.

"Look at that dinosaur," says Rico.

"Dinosaurs are old," says Robot.

Robot checks off "old" from
the list.

"Time for the next word," says
Robot. "Over."

Rico looks up. "That is over us,"
he says.

"Good one," says Robot.

Robot checks off "over" from the list.

"I see a T. rex," says Rico.

"Look at those teeth," says Robot.

"They are very big," says Rico.

Robot checks off "big" from
the list.

"Look at this one!" says Rico.

"That dinosaur is long," says Robot.

Robot checks off "long" from the list.

"This one is short," says Rico.

"It sure is," says Robot.

Robot checks off "short" from
the list.

"This one swims under the water," says Rico.

"Perfect!" says Robot.

Robot checks off "under" from the list.

"Look at those horns," says Rico.

"Horns are hard," says Robot.

Robot checks off "hard" from
the list.

"What is soft around here?"
asks Robot.

"The nest is soft," says Rico.

Robot checks off "soft" from the list.

"And the eggs are small," says Robot.

Robot checks off "small" from the list, too.

"Only one word left," says
Robot. "New."

"Look at this sign," says Rico.

Robot checks off "new" from
the list.

"Let's eat," says Rico. "That game made me hungry!"

STORY WORDS

museum   checks   horns

dinosaur   T. rex   nest

Total Word Count: 290

One robot. One boy. One crazy fun friendship! Read all the Robot and Rico adventures!

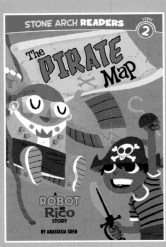